Friendship and Adventure
Storybook

**Marshall
Home Alone**

4

PUPcorn!

18

**Pups Save
the Parade**

32

studio fun

A READER'S DIGEST COMPANY

White Plains, New York • Montréal, Québec • Bath, United Kingdom

Marshall
Home Alone

It was a big day for the PAW Patrol.
Ryder was taking the pups to practice their
"pup-achute" skills high above Adventure
Bay! But Marshall really didn't like to fly.
   "Aww, that's okay, Marshall," Ryder said.
"You can stay and guard the Lookout."

"Really? Woo! Yeah!"
Marshall yelped. "I'll be the
best Lookout looker-outer
you've ever had!" He waved
good-bye to all the other pups.

Meanwhile, at Katie's Pet Parlor,
Katie was busy grooming kittens.
She was so busy she didn't see four
little kittens escape from their carrier.
Katie's cat, Cali, tried to stop them, but
it was too late. The kittens were gone!

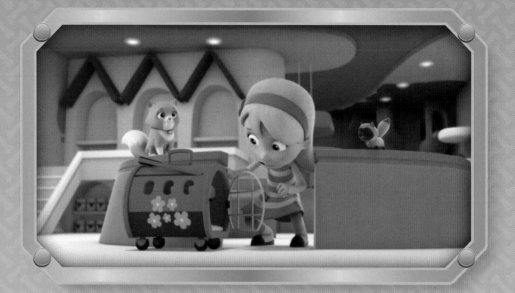

Katie turned around and saw the empty
carrier. "Oh no!" she cried. "Where did they
all go? Here kitty, kitty, kitty," Katie called.

The kittens were scampering all over Adventure Bay! But Katie knew who could help her get them back safely. "The PAW Patrol!" she said, pulling out her phone.

Katie was surprised when she found out Marshall was all alone. She wasn't sure he could save the kittens all by himself. But he assured her, "No job is too big, no pup is too small...even if he's by himself." He gathered up all the Pup Packs and headed out.

"Thanks for coming, Marshall," said Katie when he arrived in his fire truck. "One of the kitties ran down to the beach!"

Together, they sped to the beach. On the shore, they spotted a gray kitten inside a hollow driftwood log chasing a starfish that it had found. They had to figure a way to get the kitty out!

"I have the perfect tool for the job," said Marshall. He rushed to his fire truck and came back wearing Rubble's Pup Pack and helmet!

"Shovel!" he shouted, activating Rubble's tool. Marshall used the shovel to lift and tilt the log, and the kitten slid out the other side!

"Great!" said Katie. "Just three more to go!"

Just then, they saw a black-and-white kitten chasing a butterfly.

"I have the perfect tool to help us catch him," Marshall said.

Katie crept closer to the kitten as Marshall ran to his truck. When he returned, he was wearing Chase's Pup Pack and police hat.

"Marshall is on the case!" he cried. "Net!"

At his command, the net shot
from Chase's pack and caught the
second kitten—and Katie, too!

As they put the second kitty in the carrier, Marshall and Katie noticed a third kitten scampering by. It leapt onto a surfboard that started drifting into deep water!

Marshall knew what to do. He strapped on Zuma's Pup Pack with its special scuba gear. "Let's get wet!" he shouted, diving into the bay.

"Hi, kitty," said Marshall when he reached the surfboard. "Ready for a ride?"

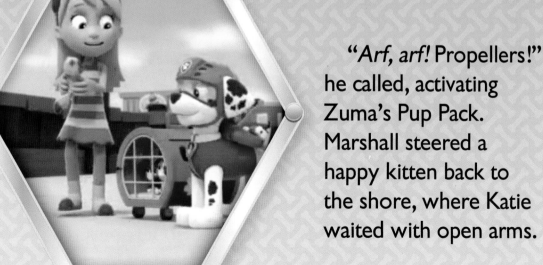

"*Arf, arf!* Propellers!" he called, activating Zuma's Pup Pack. Marshall steered a happy kitten back to the shore, where Katie waited with open arms.

Marshall and Katie spotted the last kitten walking across the bridge! They raced to the scene, and when they arrived, they saw that the kitten had begun to climb one of the bridge's cables.

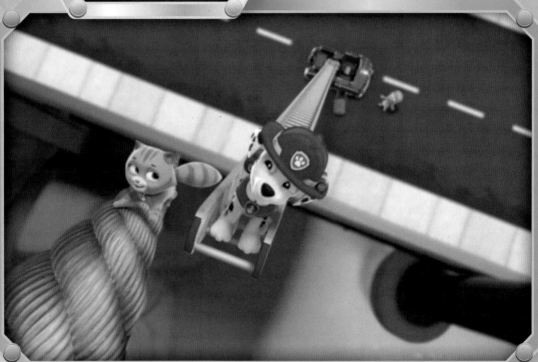

"Ladder up!" cried Marshall. He then scrambled up his fire truck's ladder, but the kitten climbed out of reach.

There was only one thing to do. Marshall donned Skye's Pup Pack, pilot goggles, and hat. Even though he was nervous about flying, Marshall knew he could do it.

"Wings!" he shouted, and out of the Pup Pack they sprang. "This pup's gotta fly!"

With that, Marshall flew to the top of the bridge and rescued the orange kitten.

Ryder and the rest of the pups returned from their pup-achute practice just in time to see Marshall swoop down and hand the kitten to Katie. They couldn't believe their eyes. Marshall was…flying!

When Marshall landed, Ryder gave him a good scratch behind the ear.

"You really did look out for the Lookout while we were gone," said Ryder. "What a good pup!" Marshall smiled. It turned out that flying wasn't so bad after all.

Back at Katie's Pet Parlor, everyone played, did backflips, and even took bubble baths. As for Marshall, he and the little orange kitten shared one last adventure together: a good nap!

PUPcorn!

Down at the farm, Farmer Al was getting ready for the big corn roast. Rubble and Rocky were by his side, helping him turn his cornfield into a giant corn maze. Rubble used his shovel to knock down the cornstalks while Rocky loaded the ears of corn onto a wagon. "The maze is a-mazing!" said Farmer Al.

"And we're going to have lots and lots of corn to roast," said Rubble. But first, they would have to shuck the corn.

Rubble and Rocky got to work helping Farmer Al. Soon piles of freshly shucked corn were everywhere. By the time they were finished, Rubble and Rocky looked like a couple of...corndogs!

Farmer Al began roasting ears of corn on the grill, and shortly after, the first guests arrived. "The only thing Chickaletta likes better than corn is grilled corn!" said Mayor Goodway.

Some of the roasted corn kernels got so hot they POPPED— and pelted Bettina.

A frightened Bettina bolted,
knocking over the grill as she ran.
Hot coals spilled onto the corn piles!
The corn began to smoke and pop!

Farmer Al knew just whom to call. "Ryder! I need the PAW Patrol's help before the corn roast turns into a bonfire!"

"Don't worry," said Ryder. "No job is too big, no pup is too small." He called all the pups to the Lookout and filled them in on the situation.

"Marshall," said Ryder, "I need you and your water cannons to put out the hot coals.

"Rubble, I need you to scoop up the dry husks and corn and move them away from the heat."

Ryder, Marshall, and Rubble raced to the farm. Marshall quickly sprang into action, spraying water on the hot coals. He prevented a fire, but the corn piles had already turned into…popcorn piles!

Just then, a worried Mayor Goodway rushed over to Ryder. "Chickaletta is lost in the corn maze!" she cried.

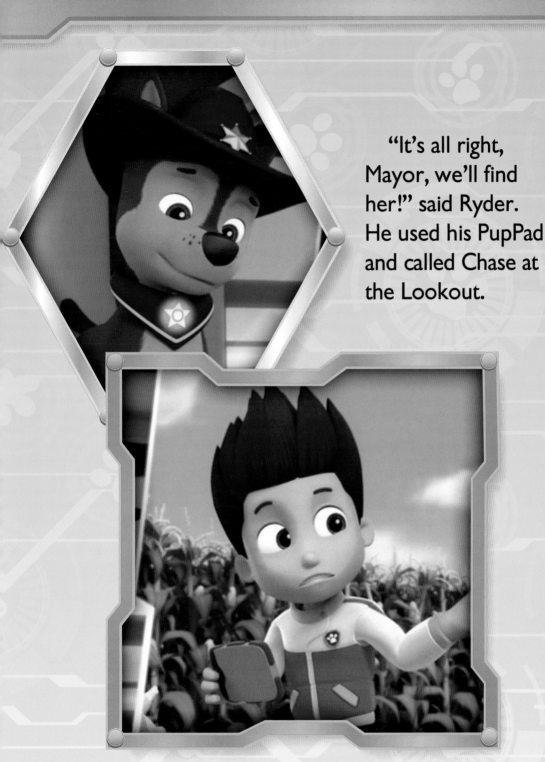

"It's all right,
Mayor, we'll find
her!" said Ryder.
He used his PupPad
and called Chase at
the Lookout.

"I need you to use your spy drone
and heat vision goggles to see if you
can spot Chickaletta," he explained.
"Super Spy Chase is on the case!"
Chase cheered.

Chase sped to the farm in his spy truck.
Once there, he called out, "Deploy!"
His drone shot into the sky and began
scanning the corn maze for Chickaletta.

Chase followed the drone's path on
a video screen. "I see her!" he cried.

"Hooray!" shouted a relieved Mayor Goodway. But just then, Chickaletta disappeared in a pile of popcorn.

"You had better go in," Ryder said to Chase. "And use your heat vision goggles to find her."

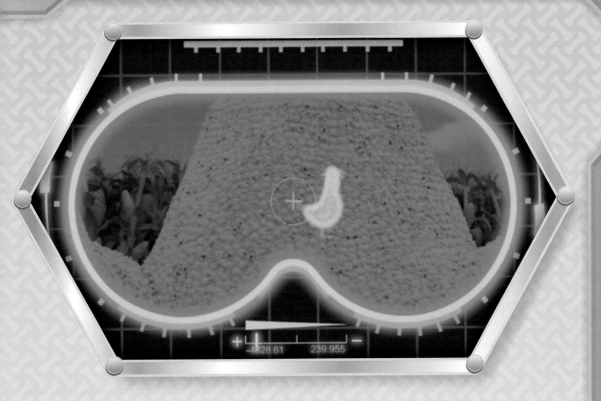

Chase hurried into the maze, and using his heat vision goggles, he located Chickaletta in the middle of a popcorn pile! He dove right in and reappeared with Chickaletta.

Chase led Chickaletta out of the corn
maze and back to Mayor Goodway.
"Chickaletta, you're safe!" the Mayor cried.

But Farmer Al
was sad. All his
corn had popped.
"The corn roast
is ruined!" he said.
Ryder looked at
the corn. "I have
an idea," he said.

Ryder sent Rubble to collect all the popcorn with his shovel. The rest of the pups helped Farmer Al put the popcorn into bags. They turned the corn roast into a popcorn festival.

And everyone had their fill of good times and fresh, pup-tacular popcorn!

Pups Save the Parade

The pups were getting ready for the Adventure Bay Day Parade. In honor of the occasion, Marshall turned his water cannons into confetti shooters!

Zuma turned his vehicle into a cool pirate float. "*Arr*, shiver me timbers, dude!" he said with a giggle.

Meanwhile, Ryder was helping get Skye's helicopter ready so she could skywrite a big surprise!

Rubble was filling the bucket loader of his Digger with gray balloons that looked like rocks...and trying to keep them from floating away.

Over on Main Street, Katie drove up
with a giant bathtub float decorated with
pink balloons that looked like bath bubbles.

Cali and
Chickaletta, each
wearing a colorful
shower cap, sat in
the huge tub.
Alex helped
Katie tie even
more balloons to
her float...

...which made it *really* begin to float! Up, up, up into the air it went!

The tub—with Cali and Chickaletta still in it—drifted away until the giant straw on top of the lemonade stand snagged it.

A frantic Mayor Goodway called Ryder on his PupPad and asked him to help. Ryder immediately called the pups to action!

"We have to save Cali and Chickaletta AND get the tub down in time for the parade," he told them.

Marshall, Chase, and Ryder
raced to the scene. "Ladder up!"
called Marshall, and he rode his fire
truck's rising ladder up to the float.

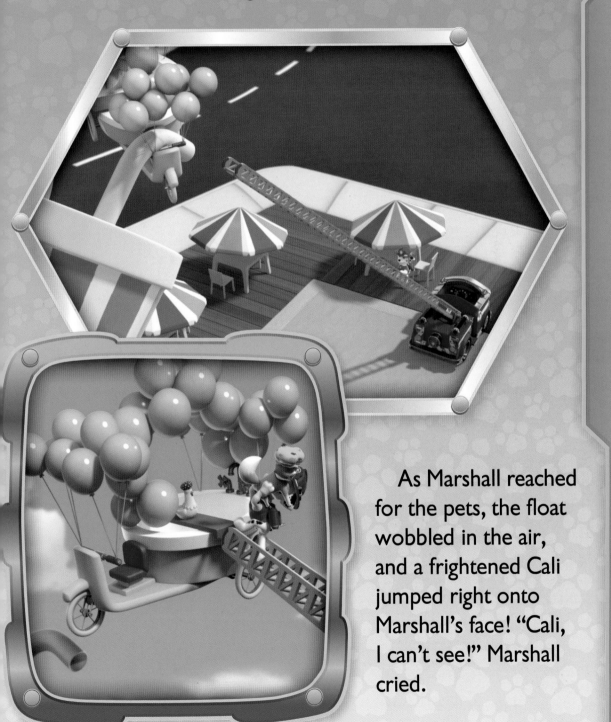

As Marshall reached
for the pets, the float
wobbled in the air,
and a frightened Cali
jumped right onto
Marshall's face! "Cali,
I can't see!" Marshall
cried.

Marshall tumbled into the floating bathtub. The force of his landing freed the float from the giant straw and it began to drift even farther away.

Marshall tried to steer the float, but bumped into giant balloons shaped like Rocky and Skye.
"Eww! A giant Rocky nose!" said Marshall.

Marshall managed to steer the float away from the giant balloons, but then the tub bumped into the tower atop City Hall and Chickaletta fell out! Everyone watching below gasped.

"Net!" Chase cried, and the cannon in his Pup Pack fired a huge net over the area. Chickaletta landed in the net and bounced safely into Mayor Goodway's arms!

"Chickaletta!" the Mayor cried with delight.

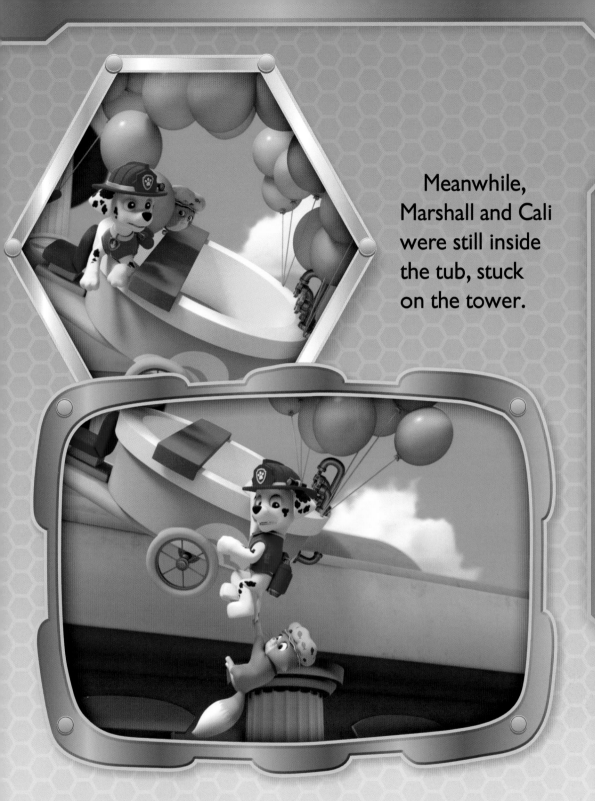

Meanwhile, Marshall and Cali were still inside the tub, stuck on the tower.

Suddenly, the wind blew, the tub tilted, and Marshall and Cali started to slide. Just in the nick of time, Marshall grabbed the tub's edge and Cali managed to hold on to Marshall's tail!

"Ryder, somebody's got to save them!" said Katie.
"We need Skye," said Ryder, and he called her on his PupPad.

"Boy, am I glad to see you!" cried Marshall as Skye swooped over to him. With Cali still clinging to his tail, Marshall used his teeth to grab the bar from Skye's helicopter. Then Skye safely piloted her copter down to the ground. Cali rushed into Katie's arms for a hug and a snuggle.

Marshall and Cali were safe, but the tub was still up in the sky floating away!

"Chase, you can shoot tennis balls from your cannon to pop some balloons!" said Ryder.

Chase began to shoot one tennis ball after another at the float. The balls hit the balloons and popped them, and ever so gently, the float sank back down to the ground.

The Adventure Bay Day Parade finally got under way. The team proudly drove down Main Street, beneath Skye's PAWsome skywriting and the giant balloons shaped like everyone's favorite pups—the PAW Patrol!